WestBow Press books may be ordered through booksellers or by contacting:

WestBow Press
A Division of Thomas Nelson & Zondervan
1663 Liberty Drive
Bloomington, IN 47403
www.westbowpress.com
1 (866) 928-1240

Because of the dynamic nature of the Internet, any web addresses or links contained in this book may have changed since publication and may no longer be valid. The views expressed in this work are solely those of the author and do not necessarily reflect the views of the publisher, and the publisher hereby disclaims any responsibility for them.

Any people depicted in stock imagery provided by Getty Images are models, and such images are being used for illustrative purposes only. Certain stock imagery © Getty Images.

ISBN: 978-1-4908-7820-1 (sc)

Library of Congress Control Number: 2015906608

Print information available on the last page.

WestBow Press rev. date: 02/23/2019

Acknowlededgments:

To those who survive, who never give up,

you inspire us all to face our challenges.

I would also like to dedicate this book

to my sister Darris, (for bravery above and beyond)

my dear friend Ruth, (who kept going and going...)

my sweet daughter in law Kristen, (scars are a

reminder that we've received our healing)

and finally to my husband Jeff.

It is a joy to be paired with you, my love!

It is a strange tale I have to tell with a highly

unlikely beginning for a princess,

but none the less true.

My life began in

a sock drawer

amongst a host of

peers, each of us with

an identical twin!

Believe me, it was

a comfortable life of

companionship.

As we all took our

turn leaving the

safety of our sock drawer home to brave new adventures

of the day, we always had our trusty twin by our side.

At the end of the day we delighted
in the society of socks, undergarments and
various clothes amongst towels and sheets
in the confines of the
hamper. Though we
weren't at our best,
and were soiled and in
desperate need of a good
scrub, we had stories still
fresh in our minds.
How we enjoyed long
talks about the happenings
of the day.

Then off to the bath, (a bit dizzying)

and the exhilarating whirl of the dryer.

(which always left me feeling flushed!)

At this stage you tend to be
separated from your twin but
this was to be expected and
we grew used to the routine.

Oh, the very best of times were on a day when the sky was blue, the breeze was balmy, & you were hung on the clothesline to dry.

It did involve a certain amount of pinching from the clothespin, but being small we only required one and after awhile you really hardly noticed the ache.

We always pitied the sheet who needed
many clothespins to hold him to the line,
although he was compensated by the wind
who would obligingly whip round and
through the sheet turning him into a mighty sail.
This delighted the children to no end!

In fact I'm sure he thought nothing
of the price he paid, for he was the center
of all the excitement and at the end of the day
was snuggled close to the children on their bed,
where they slept peacefully.

Yes, he saw so much more of the world peeking out from under the blanket. Ahh to be a sheet! And of course he had his companion. They weren't exactly the same, but worked together as a team. The fitted sheet hugged the mattress, (the mattress, I believe, was quite smitten) and the flat sheet was laid on top. When it was bedtime in the nursery, they made a lovely child sandwich!

Such a cozy place to rest.

Our place was once again in the top drawer,

paired with our twin, folded neatly together,

left to dream of

tomorrow and the

wonders it might hold.

And so our days

seemed to stretch

endlessly before us

in the comfort of

predictability.

The seasons were laid

neatly in a row as so

many socks in the top drawer.

Now a sock, like flowers and butterflies
and other beautiful things has a relatively short life span.
This is not cause for sorrow, it is merely the way things
were meant to be. Please note this life lesson
from a sock who has been there; do not be fooled
by routine, for this life is anything but
predictable, as my story will attest to and support.

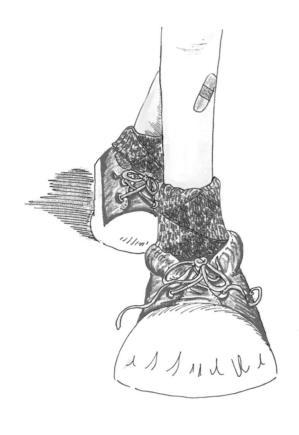

We live life at a quick pace,
always on the go and are
literally worn out!

Or in the case of a frillier variety,
seldom used and outgrown
(a pampered life to be sure. I
imagine that other than a few
parties, this life might be quite
boring, I mean, there is no place
on the playground for lace,
but I digress.)

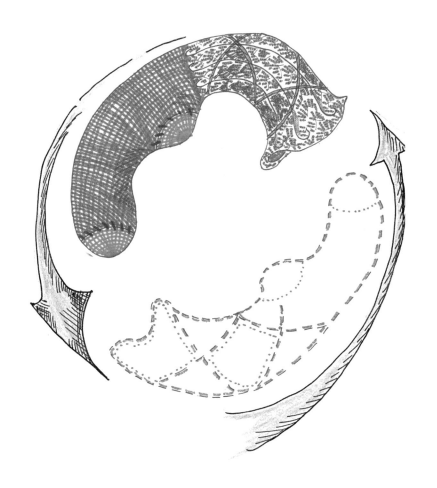

Now the exception to this natural course of events

is when the unthinkable occurs...

Somehow, through the mystery of the

regular laundry cycle, your twin disappears.

As shocking as this heinous crime was to me,

the authorities were never called in to investigate!

And here came the turn that my life was to take.

I was left to mourn my loss

in the top drawer for a week

in hopes that my partner would be found.

But, alas, this was not meant to be.

As I bid farewell to my friends in the drawer I was removed and tossed into a sack in the closet. I was soon to discover that my new home was referred to, without much ceremony, as the "rag bag". A strange place to be sure. I was in good company here and fit right in with the outcasts of the fabric society. Some were just tatters of their former selves, hardly recognizable, yet with a use. They seemed content that they still had a purpose. And, might I add, that surely they possessed an inner beauty that seemed to me to shine through their circumstances. Quite remarkable indeed!

The work we had to do when escaping the bag was hard

and messy, they informed me,

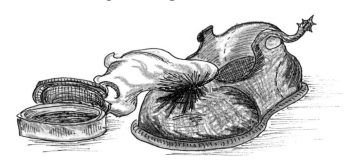

when you finished (if you survived) you were allowed

the roller coaster ride of the laundry cycle.

Then, you were returned to the rag bag until

the time you were once again, summoned and

your services were required.

I must say, it's definitely nice to be needed, but I now did

not trust the laundry and knew the danger of this cycle.

Would I too be lost? Or worse yet entrusted to

such a heavy task that, in the end,

I'd be simply discarded? I suppose there must be

an end to everything…

I awoke from a dreamless sleep to the creaking of the door being opened. Was the broom going for a sweep? I hoped so, for she always came back with an update on the happenings of the household.

Oh please, NOT the vacuum— so full of hot air...He was always boasting of his power and speed, lording it over the broom. What a lot of noise!

The sweet whisk broom,
small and humble, we
thought the hero,
for he finished up the job
at hand all neat and
tidy. I rather liked his
quiet ways. He never
made a fuss over himself.

The feather duster tickled us with
her wit and lightheartedness.
She had lived a good long life and
had seen much of the house.
She expected to be around for
many days to come.

Was I soft enough to be used as a dust cloth,
I wondered suddenly? This was the first time
my thoughts had wandered from the bag.
Maybe I was ready... which was a good thing
because just then...the bag opened!

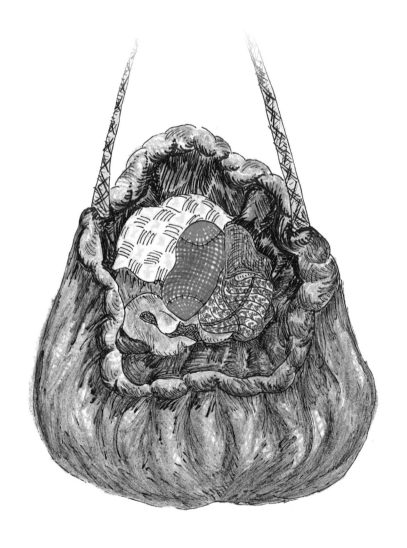

Usually a hand is thrust thoughtlessly into the bag, closing randomly upon a rag, but this time was different.

The bag was pulled open and the mistress seemed to be in search of something.

This stirred my memory of the times when just the right pair of socks were needed. And I like to believe that this was now the case, and that once again, just the right sock was being sought. It was my time to be chosen, to be pulled from the security of the bag and to take leave of the closet.

My, it was good to be out in the light and air.

Ah, the house! Not much had changed.

I had lost track of the days.

I had no idea how long I had been gone.

There are plenty of sock mottos:

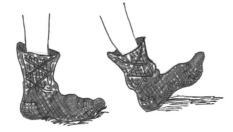

"Just put one foot in front

of the other",

"One toe over the line",

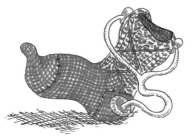

"Physician heel thyself",

and in times of extreme distress:

"Darn it!" Well, now I had a new saying:

"You just NEVER KNOW!"

For you can't be sure in that next moment what turn your life

will take, what wonders it may hold. For time keeps her secrets

close and enjoys revealing them when we least expect it.

I'll save you from the gory details. It's enough

to say that I was snipped & stitched

& with the addition of an old curtain lining,

curls & a pair of buttons,

I was born again to a new life as a sock puppet.

Held in highest esteem, I was dubbed the

"Princess of Argyle"

Argyle was the heritage I brought from my life as a sock.

Thus began my new life. Isn't it funny how just when you think

you're at the very end, it turns out to be a new beginning?

Now instead of being filled with a foot, I was carried up high

on a hand. No longer tucked in a shoe, I got to witness all the

goings on and oh my, there was plenty to be seen.

Now as all things change, it seems there was a major difference in the household. I wasn't the only one who had undergone a tremendous loss. Something was wrong. I observed that the youngest Miss was no where to be found. Had she been lost to the cycle of the laundry too!

Such a fate for one so sweet and fair. Yet, I distinctly recall the conversation in the hamper when the towel spoke at length about the washing process of the little ones and thankfully there certainly was NO mention of the dreaded washer/dryer team.

Where then was little Miss? My, she left a big hole in the family circle.

It seems the sorrow of this world had visited our happy home during my stay in the closet. Little Miss was very ill and facing the challenge of her life.

What can a simple sock do to ease her pain? I wondered. Then remembering the turn of events and the vast miracle that had transformed my life from despair to incredible fullness, I knew I had the message of hope that she desperately needed to hear, to have firmly planted in her heart. There it would grow into new life. This would be the very strength that would pull her through.

For if a mere sock could be given new life,

certainly this precious child could have the same.

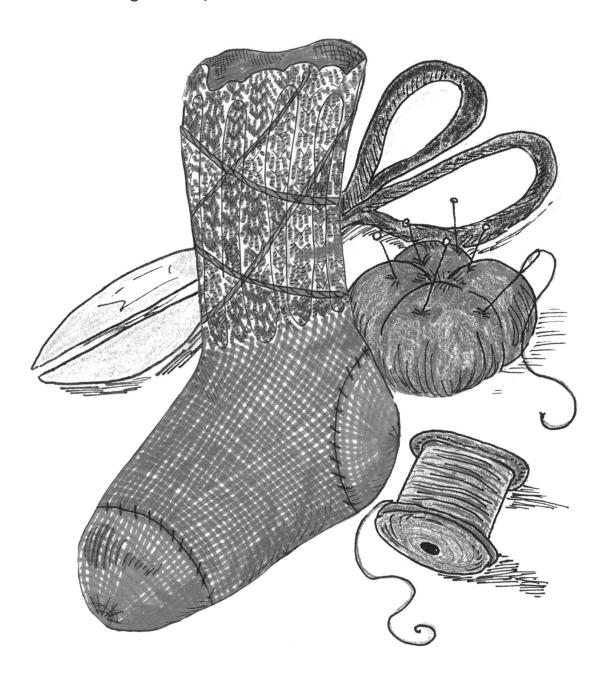

And so off we traveled. My mission was clearer than anything I'd ever known. Could button eyes truly see? Far from my life as an observer of events, I was no longer the audience to the world about me. I was about to become the entertainer, the one with a message, a story to tell.

We entered a place I had never been to before,

where sweet children, and good people

so filled with life, fought bravely to keep their own.

I saw that they too were in a sort of rag bag.

Their former lives had been taken away.

I use other people's words nowadays to amuse these little heroes, but if they could hear my thoughts I would tell of my journey, I am truly a kindred spirit! I've been in the dark, wondering what tomorrow would bring, waiting endless days.

But now I know: there is joy, even through the darkness.

Surviving is a badge of courage in itself;

life is even better after a time of testing and trial.

We shall continue, and yes we'll be changed,

I like to think for the better, we will grow and value this

life that others take for granted, Knowing how very

precious it is to be given a chance to start again!

The

Beginning!

Follow the adventures of a mismatched sock from the top drawer to parts unknown! Be encouraged and inspired to stay the course and see that all things happen for a reason, and we are never forsaken.

Darcey has been drawing before she could walk and finds it an exceptional way to communicate and express herself. She enjoys storytelling and playing with the whimsical side of life. When not playing with her beloved grandchildren and precious set of pugs, she can be found crafting with clay, sewing fiber art, or sketching and painting.

DarcArt Ink.

Printed in the United States
By Bookmasters